Hotwife to Swingers - A Multiple Partner Hotwife Romance Novel

Hot Wife Shared, Volume 3

Karly Violet

Published by Karly Violet, 2021.

Hotwife To Swingers

A Multiple Partner Hotwife Romance Novel

Sign up to my Patreon account and receive exclusive Hotwife stories every month and sexy scenes every week!

https://www.patreon.com/karlyviolet

Chapter One: Pleasure and Wanting

My wife and I walk up and down the aisles as we carry out our once-a-week grocery shopping trip at the local supermarket. We have had a relaxing weekend to ourselves and even enjoyed dining out last night at one of our favorite restaurants. It is hard to imagine having so much peace with Tonya before now.

"You are beautiful," I say to her as we stop in the cereal aisle and pick out our favorite breakfast foods.

Tonya looks at me and smiles. "Russ, that's so sweet of you to say. I don't believe you, though. I don't even have all of my makeup on this morning."

Shrugging my shoulders, I reply, "What does that matter? You have a lot of natural beauty, honey. You know that." I pull her petite body close to me and we kiss for a moment, our tongues dancing along in each other's mouths.

My wife pulls back. "Russ, we are in a supermarket at nine o'clock in the morning. Someone will see us if we don't cool down." She giggles as she puts her choice of cereal into the shopping cart.

"Someone will see us, but who cares? You let four guys have their way with you, remember?" I bend down and nibble at Tonya's ears, causing her skin to prickle and bump. My cock gets hard as I think of her old boyfriend Marcus and the way he and his investor colleagues used her as their fuck toy. Though I did not get to have the same fun with her, I still got the best seat in the house as they played with Tonya's sexy body.

"Russ, don't talk about that here," she pleads with me as her eyes grow wide. "If someone we know were to hear us..."

"Like Treena? You have been telling her about what you have been up to, haven't you?"

Tonya's face turns bright red. "That's different."

"How so? You told her that you were banging the old boyfriend. Have you told her about the other guys at the casino, Tonya? What did she say?" I fondle my wife a little after I reach under her tee shirt and find her small breasts. Her nipples are hard and responsive as I pinch each one lightly.

"Fuck, Russ." She squirms away from me as she shakes her head. "Behave yourself. You are going to get us into trouble with the management here if they catch you doing that to me."

"Maybe." I smile wickedly at my wife. "You told her, right?"

"No, I haven't," Tonya replies. "That would be a little too embarrassing."

"Too embarrassing? How is that true after you have told her about Marcus and our little agreement?" I say with a laugh. "Honey, you are getting a little too prudish on me now." Again, I approach my wife and begin to reach under her shirt.

"Okay, stop it!" she growls. I back away and begin to feel a little hurt at the response from my wife.

"Look, I'm sorry. We just can't do this here right now. I'll give you what you want when we get back home, Russ." We begin to walk down the aisle again as I shake my head. I become quiet and after a while Tonya asks me about this. "Are you sulking?"

"I'm not sulking," I tell her as I reach for something on a shelf. "I'm good, honey. Let's just get this shopping trip over."

My wife sighs. "Look, I didn't mean to be so curt with you, but you have to stop acting like a little boy in a candy store all the time. There is a place for all this and the supermarket is not it."

"But you did things like that with Marcus," I reply as I turn around to face her. "Several times, if I remember what you have told me correctly."

She nods her head. "I did, Russ. Sometimes it was a little embarrassing then, too. Don't forget that I gave you a blow job under a dining table in a restaurant a couple of months ago." Her blue eyes look hard into mine. "I'll do just about anything for you, but sometimes you push things a little too far."

"I haven't pushed anything too far yet, my love."

"Yet?" Tonya parrots as she frowns. "What is that supposed to mean? What is going on inside your head?"

I smile slightly. "Remember the conversation we had about playing around with other people? Are you still willing to let me have some of the same fun you have been having with Marcus and the other guys?"

"Russ." She shakes her head. "Do we have to talk about that right now? In the middle of an aisle in a store?"

"Why not? You said a couple of months ago that you were open to letting me have sex with another woman, but that hasn't happened yet, has it? When are we going to actually do that?"

"I don't know," Tonya replies before pursing her lips together.

"I'm not trying to be an ass or anything, but I think that we have waited long enough. Marcus is with his wife and kid and no longer wants to have sex with you, honey. Our sex life has begun to dry up again, and I can't help but think that we are letting it cool down too much. If we were to both find something fun to do..."

"You mean, like swapping with someone?" Tonya shakes her head. "We don't know anyone who would be willing to do something like that, Russ. Besides, it would be embarrassing to ask."

"And it wasn't embarrassing to fuck your boyfriend again after all these years?"

"Ex-boyfriend," Tonya stresses as she glares at me. "We had already had sex in the past before we decided to start things up again, Russ. You and I don't have anyone else in our lives who we can say that about in the same way."

"I have an old girlfriend from college," I offer. Suddenly, I get the feeling that I should have kept that comment to myself. "She's divorced now, Tonya. It would be a great way to let me get even with what you have had."

"Let me get this straight," she replies. "You want to have sex with your ex-girlfriend from years ago but not let me have someone over too?"

"You had Marcus for months," I remind her. "Why are you looking at this as being unfair? It's the same thing that you did, Tonya."

"It's *not* the same," she complains. "Not at all. You were in love with *what's-her-name*."

"Her name is Sandra."

"Sandra," Tonya chuckles. "Well, I guess if you want to go back to her..."

"What the hell has this turned into?" I say as I shake my head. "Honey, step back for a moment. I'm not going after an old girlfriend, okay? Even though it would be an even play for me. It's just that I am trying to point out that you said you were willing to think about letting me have my own bit of sexual fun, but so far you are not letting me do that. Whenever I bring it up, you change the subject or get offended." Tonya knows that I am right, but she will never admit as much. Though her initial thought after the casino trip was to let me have sex with another woman, she has sense taken a step back from that. My wife is a little more possessive than I am and apparently it has been difficult for her to consider me with anyone else. At least, that is what appears to be the case as she reaches for my shorts.

"You want to be public about this? Fine. I can do that." Tonya's soft little hand moves into my shorts and she grips my hardening member tightly.

"Shit, honey."

"Be quiet," she commands as she begins to rub my cock slowly. Breathing hard, I move closer to her as if we are talking quietly to each other.

"Oh..." I pre-come a little and Tonya uses the natural lubricant to play with the end of my manhood. My body tenses as she kisses the side of my neck.

"You want to come in the store, huh? Then I'll make you come in the store, Russ. If someone sees what we are doing, I'll blame it all on you." Though we were arguing just a moment ago, my wife seems to become playful with me as she works her fingertips over the end of my johnson. "You're going to come soon," she comments.

"Fuck, maybe we should wait until later," I say to her.

"No, Russ. You wanted this, so you are going to get it right now." She tightens her grip and pulls hard on me as if she is milking a cow. My body quivers as my breathing becomes shallower and faster.

"Shit, Tonya..."

"You probably want to try to keep it down, baby. When you come, it's going to make a mess and you don't want to attract any attention." Her hand moves faster as she anticipates that I am about to come.

"Fuck..." My body suddenly stiffens as I reach around and pull my wife hard against my body. *"Ohhhh..."* I try to be quiet as I begin to ejaculate into my shorts with Tonya's hand around my cock. *"Uhhh...ohhh...ohhh..."* I can feel my face turn deep red as I empty my balls out into my wife's hand. The idea of coming in a public store makes the intensity of the orgasm much greater and I wonder if I might yell out too loudly. Thankfully, I am able to control myself as I finish losing my wad.

Tonya pulls her hand out of my shorts and wipes it off with a small Kleenex from her purse. "You were a very messy boy, Russ," she jokes playfully as she tosses the spent tissue paper into the cart.

"I need something," I say to her as I look down at my leg. "Honey, it's dribbling down my leg. Help me." Worried that someone could see me, I look around for other shoppers nearby. An older woman walks past the aisle with her cart, but she barely glances at us before continuing along her way.

"I don't have another tissue," Tonya replies. "You made the mess, sweetheart. You are going to have to clean it up."

I look around the aisle and see a package of dish towels near the dishwashing liquid. I grab the package and after opening it I use one to wipe up the trail of jism running down my leg. I also reach into my shorts to retrieve the mess that is still inside. My face contorts as I think about how much semen I have inside my underwear and shorts at the moment.

"I told you that we should have waited until we got home, Russ. You insisted, though."

"And you have more tissues," I grumble as we begin to move again. "I know you do."

"Maybe," she giggles. "Still, you are going to have to pay for those dish towels. I would suggest that you come up with some kind of lie about why you opened them up and used one."

Goosebumps rise along the back of my neck. *"Fuck."*

"Yep. Fuck." Tonya laughs as we make our way to the next aisle. Though there are still some sticky remnants of my spilled ball juice inside my shorts, I can't help but smile with her. She gave me what I wanted, even though she knew what would happen when she did. My wife is good like that. She can take whatever I claim to want and turn it around on me. As a matter of fact, I would bet that she might do the same when it comes to my request to have sex with another woman. Bringing up Sandra the way she did was a warning to me not to get too carried away with the thought that I can have the same fun with another woman that she had with her ex-boyfriend Marcus. Tonya is right. What she had with him is different than what I had with Sandra. That being said, I would still love to bury my cock in Sandra one more time.

Chapter Two: A Friend's Advice

"Hey, buddy, what's the word?" One of my best friends and a colleague at work, Theo, walks into my office and closes the door behind him. He sits down opposite my desk and puts his feet up on the surface.

"Um, alright. Go ahead and put your damned feet on my desk," I chuckle while shaking my head.

Theo puts his feet down on the floor as he smiles at me. "Just looking for a place to relax, Russ. So, what the hell is up with you? I haven't seen you eating in the cafeteria in a long time."

"Well, I've been trying to have lunch with Tonya almost every day," I reply as I sit forward and put my forearms on my desk.

"Oh, really? Things are going that well that you are taking time to eat with the wifey?"

I laugh. "Things are actually pretty good, yeah. We have our ups and downs, but things have really been up lately." I smile at my friend as I nod my head. Theo knows me better than anyone else besides Tonya.

"I'm glad to hear that. So, the thing on the side is still good?" He allows a devilish grin as he references what I have told him about Tonya and Marcus. It has been some time since I have updated Theo on what has been going on, which has been somewhat on purpose for my part. It is probably part of the reason that I spend lunch with my wife as well.

"It's over," I say as I shake my head. "Tonya and her old boyfriend agreed that it was time to finally break things off. So, they don't plan to see each other anymore."

"No shit?" Theo shakes his head as if he is supremely disappointed at the news.

"No shit," I confirm. "I think it is probably for the best. The guy has a wife and daughter at home and he was getting a little nervous about how she felt about the arrangement."

"But I thought you said that his wife was fine with it all?"

"She was," I reply. "But after some time, she was beginning to worry that he might up and fall for Tonya. So, they broke things off and now Tonya and I are monogamous once again." I feign a smile as I think about just how much I hate hearing myself say that. Though monogamous was precisely what we declared we would be during our wedding vows, it is not the sort of relationship that I would now prefer. Over the last several months, I have learned that my sexual appetite, as well as Tonya's, is much larger than I had previously thought.

"Well, damn. That sort of dampens things for me. You were really keeping me happy with the little updates you were giving me." Though I have told Theo very little, he did enjoy hearing about some of the situations where the sex was occurring.

"The casino was great," I tell him. "She had sex with four guys at once."

"Yeah, you told me," he laughs. "That was the last thing that you told me. I was hoping to come in here today and hear that she had a gangbang." I laugh with my friend as I shake my head. "That is not the sort of thing that Tonya would be happy with. As a matter of fact, I don't think she is happy about the idea of me having sex with another woman at all right now."

"She's backing out?"

"Probably. I mean, Tonya was good with the idea right after the casino thing, but now she acts like I am talking about cheating on her. Why has she changed her mind?"

"Women," Theo tells me with a straight face. "I was married for a while to a real bitch, remember? She didn't want to do anything with me in bed, but it didn't take much at all for another man to convince her to shag him. Out of all that tom-fuckery, though, there is one bright spot that I do remember. She tried to get me to go to a swingers club with her."

"A swingers club?" I shake my head as I look over at Theo. "Are you serious? She *wanted* to go?"

"Sure she did," he laughs. "Her lover was going to be there on a certain night and she saw it as an opportunity to screw him. Though I thought about agreeing to go, I found out about the other guy before we could finalize the plans. That essentially threw everything out the window." Theo scowls as he sits back in his chair. "Honestly, I think we would have had a great time if she had just not cheated on me, Russ."

"A swingers club. I wonder what Tonya would think about that idea?"

"I would be careful with that," my friend warns. "If she is already hesitant about letting you have sex with someone else, that could turn into a disaster for you."

"If she were to agree to go, how would she be upset with me for having sex with someone else?"

Theo shakes his head. "Women have their own thoughts on things. What you see as fair does not necessarily seem fair to someone like Tonya. Russ, you have to be careful to make sure that whatever she needs or wants is tied into whatever *you* need or want. If you do not both agree to what that is, you can't just go and have sex with some other woman. It would royally piss her off."

"Like the way she went behind my back to sext with her old boyfriend?" I say defensively. "It doesn't really seem fair, man."

"It's not fair. It's not supposed to be." Theo smiles. "Look, I know you better than you know yourself. You love Tonya more than anything in the world and you want to make her happy. So, don't screw things up with her just because you are a little horny. If you want to look into a swingers club, do that, but don't go there and get laid by yourself." He pauses and adds, "I don't think you can go as a single guy anyway. Everybody has to bring a wife or a date in most clubs."

"And they cost to get into, right?"

He nods his head. "Most of them do, I think. They have membership fees that weed out the serious ones from the horny guys just looking for things online. The fees also pay for things like a background check. At least, that's how the one we were going to go to did things."

"Where was that club at?" I ask as I think about how much fun it would be to go to one with Tonya.

"It's here in the city," he replies. "I believe it is also the only one locally. You want one that has a good, clean reputation, and this place has that."

My heart begins to race as I think about how exciting it would be to swap my wife for another woman for a little fun. Would this be something that Tonya could agree to try? Maybe so, but I need to know more before I go and try to convince my wife that we should join any swingers club.

"Do you happen to know the name of the club?" I ask.

Theo smiles. "I don't walk around with that in my mind, buddy. I'll try to find the old email I got from them a few years ago and forward it to you later. To be honest, when I divorced the old lady I just forgot all about that place. There's no reason to swing without a partner."

"Aren't you seeing someone right now, though?"

"Kathryn," he replies. "She is definitely not the type to do something like that, though. So, no, I won't be going to a swingers club or anywhere else for sex right now. I'm happy with what I have with her." Theo has been in a much better mood around work since meeting Kathryn at a singles retreat a couple of months back. Whatever she is doing for him, it is working wonders for his attitude.

"So, you send me that information when you get a chance and I'll look it up," I tell him. "Maybe I can get Tonya to agree to do something like that with me."

"Maybe. Just work it carefully, Russ. You know how your wife can be if you try to cram this down her throat." He makes a vulgar motion with his hand as his tongue moves along the inside of his cheek.

"Fuck, man," I say with a laugh as I shake my head. "She didn't have any trouble with that when she was seeing Marcus."

"And it's gotten better for you since then, right?"

Smiling, I nod my head. "Well, yeah, it's gotten a lot better. I'm trying to keep the fire going, though. Things have slowed down for us a little and I don't want it to burn out on us."

"Good time to see about the club, then, huh?" Theo smiles at me again. "Well, I need to get back to my office. I have a presentation to turn in to Brady and some of the others upstairs. If you need anything, just let me know. You know that I support you in your sexual endeavors, brother." We both laugh as he stands to his feet.

"Just get that information to me, alright? That would be great." Theo nods his head and turns toward the door. He soon leaves my office and I begin to think over the idea of going to a swingers club with Tonya.

"Would you go?" I ask as I think about her slight aversion to me having sex with another woman. We have talked about me having sex with someone else and I thought my wife was completely on board with the idea, but as we have gotten further from when she had sex at the casino Tonya has changed her mind. It is difficult to know why this has happened, though I have tried to understand better her view on it all. Asking her about it only seems to bother my wife. I do not want to annoy her, but I do want to make her aware of the fact that she has previously told me that things would change and that I would get the same consideration from her that I have given.

"Dammit." I take a quick breath as I think about how difficult it could be to convince Tonya to take a look at the swingers club with me. Though she will probably be turned on by the prospect of having sex with other men, my wife is likely to be cool to the idea of me doing the same with other women. There does not seem to be an easy way to convince her either, which is aggravating as I think about where to go from here.

"The information first," I tell myself as I think about Theo's promise to forward the email to me. "Then a plan." I sit back in my chair and look on the computer screen to my left. There is no email from my old friend yet, but soon I expect there will be. Afterwards, I will begin to make plans for how I will approach Tonya about this idea.

Chapter Three: Something to Consider

Theo makes good on his promise and later in the afternoon sends me a copy of his original email with the managers of a swingers club in town. As I sit at my desk, I consider what to say to them as I prepare my own email to them.

"Shit, I'm shaking like a leaf," I say to myself as I think about what I will say to the club management. "I don't know them." Though I am incredibly turned on by the idea of going to a swingers club with my wife, I am a bit more shy when it comes to initiating this sort of thing. Attempting to keep my message as professional as I possibly can, I tell them that I am interested in the club but that I would like more information. As I send the email off, I feel my heart beat hard for a moment while I consider what sort of response I will likely get in return.

I get back to work on several tasks as I try to forget about the email. This works for a while as I fill out forms for a purchase order and then forward them to the accounting department. In between the forms, I take a quick look at my personal email and notice that I have gotten a reply to the email I sent to the swingers club management. "Oh, wow." Breathing deeply and trying to keep my head level, I open it up and begin to read.

"Hello, Russ! This is Chelsea Hanover and I am one of the managers at our little club. It is great to see that you are interested in our little nest of fun!" She seems very chipper as she begins her email to me. Getting a little hard, I continue to read. "We are a safe place for couples to explore each other and the partners of others in a warm, inviting private home. Located in the downtown area, our home is safe and secure behind the gates of a private community. Those who apply are screened and required to sign nondisclosure agreements in order to be a part of any of the events here. We love to meet new couples and I am sure that you and your significant other would have a great time with us. If you don't mind, I would prefer that you call me when you get the chance. I would like to tell you a little more about our club and what we do here." Chelsea gives a local phone number before closing out the email. I sit back in my chair and wonder what I should do next.

"I wonder if Theo ever got one of these emails?" I say to myself as I look at my office door. I want badly to go get him in here to let him read this email, but instead, I pick up my cell phone and begin to dial the number sent to me. "I can't believe that I'm doing this." As the phone rings on the other end, I put mine on speaker and lock my office door.

"Hello?"

"Um, hello, this is Russ. May I speak to Chelsea?"

"Oh, hello, Russ!" The voice on the phone is smooth and sexy, the tone causing me to get a little hard as I listen to her.

"Hello. I guess I would love to hear a little more about the club."

"Great! So, tell me, how did you hear about us?"

I swallow hard. "I have a friend who contacted you a few years ago. He never actually went with his wife, but he thought that I might be interested."

"Oh, really? Are you married or do you have a girlfriend, Russ?" My cock continues to stiffen as I listen to her voice. It surprises me that I am so horny for a woman I have never met simply because of the sound of her voice.

"I'm married," I reply. "For about three years now."

"Very nice. And, what is her name?"

"Tonya," I tell her. "I haven't convinced her yet that we should do this, so I am just getting my ducks in a row to try to get her onboard."

"Oh, I see." I detect a faint giggle on the other end of the line. "Well, let's talk about why you want to join our club and maybe I can give you some ideas to help with convincing your wife, alright?" Chelsea pauses before asking, "What is it that makes you want to go to a swingers club, Russ?"

I take a breath and think about this for a moment. There are a flurry of reasons that I can think of, but the one that sticks out most is what I tell her. "My wife has been having sex with an old boyfriend of hers.

I know and I approve, but now we are considering letting me have the same sort of fun. So, I think it would be great if we were to both be able to trade off with some other people so that we can both be with each other while this happens. Though we have experimented a little, I don't think we want to go too sexually crazy, if you know what I mean."

"I know exactly what you mean," Chelsea replies. "The scenario you have told me about is not that different than some of the others I have heard over the years. It's often true that one or the other in the relationship is already active sexually with someone else and they want to involve the other partner. So, they come to us and we are able to help them with that most of the time. Tell me, Russ, what do you like during sex?"

"During sex?" The question takes me a little by surprise. "I don't know. I guess I like to get off, to be honest." We both laugh at my answer, but it is not quite enough to satisfy Chelsea.

"What do you like, though? Tell me everything.z

"Um, okay?" My face begins to burn as I get a little embarrassed. "Well, I guess I like a little of everything. I am definitely an oral guy; I love to give and receive. I also love to try different positions."

"Would you call yourself sexually adventurous?" she asks.

I nod my head. "I think so. I mean, I like new things and so does my wife. The problem is finding other people to do those new things with."

"And we can help with that," Chelsea replies. "Can you do me a favor, Russ?"

"Sure," I reply.

"Where are you?"

"At work."

"Alone?"

"In my office."

"Good." She pauses momentarily before asking, "Could you pull your penis out of your pants?"

I sit for a moment and allow the request to process before answering, "Um, what?"

"Pull your penis out and hold it in one of your hands."

"Okay, but…"

"It's alright, Russ. You are safe with me. I can't see it and you are in your office away from other people. I do this with all the men who contact our club."

"Okay." My hand shakes a little as I unzip my pants and open them up. After I pull out my hard wanker, I look at the phone and say to her, "I have it out now."

"Very good." Chelsea seems very pleased as she tells me, "Please start to rub it as if you are going to masturbate, Russ."

"Okay." I do as she asks and my body tenses as I think about the fact that I am playing with myself at the behest of a woman I have never seen or met.

"How big are you?"

"Well, um, around seven or eight inches," I tell her.

Chelsea giggles. "Are you not certain of the exact size of your own penis?"

"Not really. I've never actually measured it." I pre-come a little as my hand squeezes my hard, throbbing manhood.

"But you think seven or eight?"

"Yeah."

"Describe it to me," Chelsea says into the phone.

"I don't know how to do that," I tell her. "It's long and hard. There is a lot of blood in it right now."

"Is it veiny?" she asks.

"Yeah, very veiny."

"And is the head really red?"

I look at the end of my cock. "Honestly, it's almost purple because I am so horny right now." I can't believe that I have admitted to Chelsea that I am really horny. Goosebumps begin to form along my arms and neck as I choke my chicken.

"Does it feel good to play with it?" she asks.

"Yeah," I reply as I begin to breathe hard.

"And, is it turning you on to tell me about it while you stroke it, Russ?" Chelsea begins to breathe hard into the phone.

"It turns me on," I admit. "A lot."

"Does it turn you on to know that I am fingering myself right now? While you are playing with your hard cock, I am rubbing my clit, Russ. Are you turned on by that?" The woman on the phone squeaks a little as she asks the question.

"Fuck, are you really doing that to yourself?"

"Of course I am," she moans. "Tell me what is happening to you, Russ. Tell me as you come what is going on."

I nod my head. "I can feel my balls aching," I say as I breathe hard. "My come is moving into my cock and I think I will probably shoot off soon. I'm pre-coming a whole lot and thinking about what it would be like to have you lick it off my dick."

Chelsea giggles. "Maybe if you join the club I can do that for you, Russ. Tell me more."

"Oh, shit," I say as I try to control myself. I don't want to ejaculate too soon. I want the woman on the other end of the line to come with me. "I'm trying to hold it, but I am going to lose it, Chelsea."

"Lose it," she encourages me. "Just come, Russ. Tell me all about it."

"I'm starting to feel it come. Chelsea...*uhhhh*..." I begin to spurt wildly into the air, some of my creamy sauce landing on top of my desk next to my cell phone. *"Ahhh...fuck...OHHHH!!!"* I imagine the woman on the other end of the line coming with me as I lose myself to the orgasm.

"It feels good, huh?" she says to me as she moans. "Russ, are you making a mess?"

"Yes...fuck..." I keep shooting off until I empty my balls into my hand and all over my lap and desktop. Taking a slow breath, I begin to clean myself up with some tissues from a box on my desk.

"How do you feel?" Chelsea asks.

"Did you come?" I reply.

"No," she giggles. "I lied a little, Russ. I wasn't playing with myself, but I wanted to make sure that you are serious about this."

"What?" I am a little irritated to discover that the whole thing was a ruse of sorts. "You told me that you were playing with yourself."

"I needed to know that you could at least come while on the phone with a stranger," she replies. "Russ, you would probably be surprised to know that about half the guys I talk to on the phone can't even do that. If you can't perform on the phone with a stranger, there is no way that you will do well with a stranger at one of our parties. The last thing we want here is to see someone fail at this once they sign up for it. It's just too much money to invest."

"How much money?" I ask as I finish cleaning up my mess.

"A thousand dollars per couple," Chelsea replies. "It covers costs such as incidentals and insurance. It's good for the entire year, but you would have to pay it again next year when your membership is renewed."

"Wow." The money in and of itself is not the problem. The problem would be getting my wife to agree to join a swingers club. "I will have to convince my wife."

"You do that. In the meantime, I will email you some additional information. If you think that your wife would like to come take a look at where the parties happen, we can set up a tour of our home. Does that sound like a good plan to you?"

I nod my head. "I think so."

"Good." Chelsea does something on the other end of the line. "I will talk to you later, then, Russ. Have a good afternoon. I look forward to seeing the two of you here."

"Thank you." We hang up from the call and I consider what has just happened. Masturbating while another woman is on the phone line is not the sort of thing that I have ever done before today. This is a first for me, and I am hopeful that I will soon experience another first by joining a swingers club with my wife. There is a lot to do to convince Tonya, though. I had better get to work figuring out just how I will present this idea to her.

Sign up to my Patreon account and receive exclusive Hotwife stories every month and sexy scenes every week!

https://www.patreon.com/karlyviolet

Chapter Four: An Excited Hubby

I keep thinking about what Russ wants and I keep coming back to the same selfish conclusion. Though I have had sex with Marcus and other men recently, I am having a hard time agreeing to my husband doing the same thing with another woman. I know this is not exactly fair, but it is just the way that I feel. For my part, I was able to detach my emotions from the sexual enjoyment I got out of being with other men. However, Russ is a loving man and I find it hard to imagine him having sex with anyone else without forming some sort of emotional attachment. It happened to us when we first had sex on our third date, so I know it is a real issue for him.

"Hey, honey," Russ says as he walks through the front door of our house. I am sitting down on the sofa and watching television as I eat a bowl of spaghetti that I reheated from the night before.

"You're home a little late," I reply. "Were things busy on your end of the building?"

"In a way," he says as he bends down and gives me a kiss. "I'm famished. Is there any more spaghetti from last night left in the refrigerator?"

"Another serving," I reply. "Help yourself." Looking up, I continue to watch the program on the television as Russ heats up some of the leftovers in the microwave. After he finishes, he makes his way to the living room and has a seat nearby.

"Good stuff," my husband says before taking his first bite.

"Yeah, I was just happy that we didn't have to cook tonight."

"You mean that *you're* happy that you didn't have to cook tonight," he says with a laugh.

"Alright, Russ, I know it was my turn. I'll cook tomorrow night, I promise. I just didn't want to let the spaghetti go to waste."

"That's fine. I look forward to your meal tomorrow night." He winks at me and smiles before turning his attention to the television as well.

"Um, what's up, sweetheart?" I say as I look over at my husband. "You seem to be really happy this evening."

Russ shrugs his shoulders. "It's been a good day, that's all. Things have been working out really well for me at work."

"Really?" I nod my head as I study my husband's facial expression. He gets happy about a lot of things, but work is often not one of them. Growing more curious about his state of emotion at the moment, I ask him, "Did you get a blow job at work?"

Russ nearly chokes on a bite of spaghetti. "Really, Tonya? Did you just ask me that?" He laughs as he puts his fork down in the bowl of pasta.

I smile at him. "You look like a guy who has gotten off, my love. What happened that put you into such a good mood today? Did you get a pay raise or a promotion?" Russ is not up for a pay increase until later in the year and I have not heard of a new position opening up inside the company. So, I doubt that either of my guesses are correct.

Russ looks at me warily before answering, "We have been talking about what we might want to do now that you and Marcus are not an item, right? Well, I might have found the answer to that question."

"Really?"

"Yeah. I emailed a place in the city earlier today and got a response. I like what I read and when I called them for more information I liked it even more."

"What is it?" My skin crawls as I think about what Russ and I have been talking about. Whatever he has found out has got to have something to do with sex.

He sighs and puts his bowl of spaghetti down on the coffee table in front of him. "Just keep an open mind, alright?" I nod my head at my husband. "There is a swingers club in the city and they want us to consider joining them."

My heart nearly jumps into my throat as I put my fork down in my spaghetti bowl. "A *swingers* club? You contacted a swingers club, Russ?"

"I was just interested, that's all," he tells me. "I didn't tell them I wanted to join for certain, honey. They seem like a very nice group of people, and Chelsea has even invited us to come tour where they hold the parties."

"Russ, I can't believe that you have been up to this." I laugh nervously as I sit forward on the sofa. "When did you decide to contact them?"

He looks uneasily at me. "It was Theo's idea."

"Oh, shit," I say as I feel goosebumps on the back of my neck. "Have you been telling him about us, Russ?"

"Only the same sort of things that you have told to your friend, honey."

"Treena is like a sister to me," I reply. "She is much better at keeping secrets than any of your buddies are."

"Theo is a very close friend of mine. He is exactly what I would hope a brother would be like for me, Tonya. If you are telling Treena about what we have been doing, then I can tell Theo."

"That's embarrassing," I say as I put my bowl of spaghetti down near his. "He suggested that you call the swingers people?"

"It was something that he and his ex-wife wanted to do before they divorced. He never went, but he still had their email address. Tonya, this could be a lot of fun for both of us, don't you think?" I can see by the sincerity in my husband's eyes that he very much believes that statement. Unfortunately, I am having a hard time seeing things his way.

"A swingers club is disgusting, Russ," I tell him. "I've seen videos of places like that. People are all over each other and things just get crazy."

"Do you mean like what happened at the casino between you and those four guys?" The reply hurts as I shake my head and just consider his response. "I'm sorry," Russ says as he realizes he has swung below the belt with me. "I shouldn't be such an asshole, but this is a great opportunity. For one thing, it is definitely not an orgy, Tonya. Chelsea told me that they are very discreet and that they screen everyone who applies. They don't allow the riff-raff in and they keep things civil between couples. Single people are not allowed to come without a sex partner."

"That's creepy, don't you think? Russ, you are talking about having sex with people that you haven't met before."

"Like three of the men you were with?" he fires back. My husband is not about to allow me to forget what I have done and the fact that he allowed it to happen for my sake.

"Russ, it just seems so odd." Shaking my head, I ask, "What do you know about this place?" He smiles a little as he sees his chance to try to convince me to consider this the club.

"Like I said, they are discrete and they do a background check. If you pass, they want a thousand dollars for a year's dues. It pays the expenses for hosting the parties. The parties are typically small, maybe a dozen couples at most at any one time, and they are very respectful. Chelsea promised me in an email she sent that if either of us are uncomfortable with anything, we don't have to take part. That seems like a good thing to me." Russ smiles widely before continuing, "They have nice bedrooms that each have at least two king size beds and showers in every room. The house is huge and they are in a gated community. You see, this is not something that is disgusting or dirty, Tonya. It is a respectable place." My husband takes a quick breath and sits back in his chair as he allows what he has told me to sink in for a moment.

I nod my head. "Alright. Let's say that I were to agree to check into this with you. You are not saying that I have to do this, right? I only need to consider it."

"Consider it with an open mind, yes," he replies. "I know you are worried about me having sex with another woman, but I think it would be something that you could enjoy as well. Remember, it would mean that you and I would essentially trade off with another couple."

"Yeah, another couple that we don't know."

"You said so yourself the other day that we don't know anyone to do that sort of thing with, Tonya. This gives us the opportunity to try this out without worrying about who it is and who will know. They have everyone sign NDA's to keep things tight-lipped."

"Wow, that's a little intense," I laugh. "NDA's?" Russ nods his head. "Maybe it would be something worthwhile to look into. I mean, it wouldn't hurt to take a tour and to hear a little more about it, huh?"

"That's what I am saying," my husband replies with a huge smile on his face. Russ's Cheshire cat smile is a little irritating, but I understand why he is so excited. I am essentially agreeing to at least look into doing something that I thought I would not do just a few days ago.

"Fine. Set up the appointment to tour the place. I'll keep an open mind and look it over with you."

"Really?" Russ nods his head before pulling his phone out of his pocket. He begins to compose a text message.

"Wait," I say as I look at him. "You have her phone number?"

"Well, yeah," he replies. "I told you that I spoke with her on the phone earlier, Tonya." Russ looks back down and continues composing the message as I stare at him. There is something about this whole thing that he has not told me, but I cannot seem to put my finger on it. Though I want to be suspicious, and in general I am, I also cannot ignore how happy this has made my husband. For that, I feel a bit proud. I like to make Russ happy and if he wants to visit a house to be happy, far be it from me to deny him that.

"The weekend would be best," I mention to him.

"Yeah, I asked about Saturday," Russ tells me as he looks up from his cell phone. "I'll let you know what Chelsea says when she replies." My husband picks his bowl of spaghetti up and begins to eat again. I do the same as I wonder what is going on inside his head. I know he wants badly to join this swingers club, but it will take a bit more to convince me that doing so would be in our best interest. Until then, I will look forward to the visit this weekend and try to keep an open mind for Russ.

Chapter Five: A Little Give and Take

34

"Good morning," a very attractive forty-something woman says to us at the front door of the large house. "I'm Chelsea." I look at the beautiful brown shoulder-length hair that flows down her face and neck. Her dark eyes are alluring as she looks seductively at me.

"I'm Russ," I reply before introducing my wife. "Tonya, this is one of the managers of the club."

"Very nice to meet you." She shakes each of our hands before allowing us into her home. As the woman closes the door behind us, she says, "My husband will be with us shortly. Please follow me to the living room." Tonya and I follow Chelsea and soon find ourselves in what must be the formal living room.

"This is a very nice house," Tonya says as we sit on a sofa beside each other.

"Thank you. Adrian and I had it built almost ten years ago when the neighborhood was coming together. Thankfully, our investment has more than tripled in value since then."

"Oh, my love, you are being a little show-offish with that stuff." I turn to see a man walking down a set of stairs nearby. He is handsome, tall, and muscular. These traits are the sort that definitely get Tonya's attention as she looks over at him.

"It's a nice home," Chelsea says to him before saying to us, "This is my husband, Adrian. Adrian, this is Russ and Tonya."

"Ah, I have heard a little about you," he says as he offers his hand to shake. After I shake hands with him, he turns to my wife and does the same, though it appears that he spends a little more time holding her hand than he did mine. There is a definite connection between the two of them, which causes me to second guess my decision to bring Tonya here.

"So, what about this club?" Tonya turns to focus her eyes on Chelsea as Adrian sits down nearby. "Russ seems convinced."

"Good," our host says with a smile. "I was hoping after our phone call the other day that he would be convinced to visit." My face turns red as

Chelsea looks at me. I have not told my wife about masturbating while on the phone with the other woman because I cannot be certain how she would react. Chelsea seems to notice my uneasiness and stays away from that bit of information.

"The club is an idea that we had a few years ago when we began to experiment ourselves," Adrian says with a smile. "Chelsea and I tried a few other places, but they were all either too small or too impersonal. Someone in one of the groups happened to mention that they would like to be a part of something that would happen in a home, and so that's how we got started. Since then, we have seen our membership grow to about fifty couples."

"Wow," I reply with a chuckle. "Fifty grand each year just from membership dues."

"It covers insurance and other things," Chelsea reminds me. "We don't make a profit from this. We don't need to." She looks over at her husband.

"We are independently wealthy," he informs us. "I have a lot of stock in some things that have taken off, so I retired early. Here I am, forty five years old, and I will not have to work the rest of my life." Adrian smiles before adding, "That's why striking early is so important. Do you own any stock?"

I look at Tonya before replying, "We have some. Tonya is invested in a company in the city as well."

"Good," he says with a nod of his head. "It's important to do that sort of thing if you want to knock off from a career early."

"Enough talk of stocks," Chelsea says as she brushes some of her brown hair over her right ear. "Let me take you around the house so that you can see where things happen during parties." She gets up from her set as do Tonya and I.

"I'll stay here," Adrian says. "Enjoy the tour." He winks at my wife and causes her to blush as we turn to follow his wife.

"Don't mind him," Chelsea laughs as she walks alongside Tonya. "My husband is an insatiable flirt. He doesn't mean anything by it, unless you want him to."

"He seems like a very nice man," Tonya replies. "Very flirtatious, like you said."

We walk down a long hallway before coming to a large room. "This is our movie theater," Chelsea tells us. "We sometimes get the parties started here. Some of our members like to watch a movie while they play around with each other." Our host points at the large screen on the wall. "Everything is high definition and in surround sound. Nothing but the best for our members." She then leads us through the theater to the other side and out through a door. There is another hallway, this one with bedrooms lined along the way.

"Here we are," Chelsea says as she leads us through an open door into a large bedroom.

"Where is the door?" Tonya asks.

"There are no doors on the bedrooms here," she tells my wife. "Everyone must be in agreement that they are okay with anyone and everyone watching them have sex."

"Everyone?" Tonya looks nervously at me.

"Honey, I don't think you will really care who is watching if you are having fun with someone." I reach over and put my arm around her shoulders. "Besides, we would be having sex with just one other couple."

"That is generally true," Chelsea says. "We discourage the orgy mentality here. It just wouldn't be the sort of reputation that we want to cultivate in our club."

"But, they can watch?"

"Yes, they can watch whenever they like. The same would be true for you and your husband, Tonya. Everyone is allowed to watch or participate. It's whatever you feel comfortable with." Chelsea walks up to Tonya and puts her hand on her shoulder. "Please don't worry, sweetie. If you want to just watch, you can just watch. There is never any pressure."

Tonya nods her head. "That's good to know." My wife manages a smile before we follow Chelsea out of the bedroom. We make our way back through the large movie theater and then to the living room where Adrian is still waiting. Something is different about him, though. I jump a little as I see that he has pulled his cock out of his pants and is stroking it.

"We would like to ask you to do something, if you don't mind," Chelsea says to us. "Tonya, would you mind giving my husband a nice blow job?"

"*What?*" My wife looks over at Adrian and then at me and Chelsea. "Are you serious?"

"You don't have to," Chelsea assures her. "But, it would go a long way to helping us see you as a part of our club." The woman turns and looks at me. "I will give you one at the same time, Russ. It is only fair that the trade is even."

"Tonya, are you okay with this?" She looks at me and then at Adrian. Tonya then goes to her knees and takes the other man's hard johnson into her hands. After stroking it slowly a couple of times, she puts her lips to his dick and slowly allows it to pass into her mouth. Adrian closes his eyes and enjoys the feeling of her wet tongue and lips on him.

"Over here," Chelsea says as she guides me to a chair nearby. She unfastens my belt and pulls my pants and underwear down before I sit down. The beautiful woman wastes no time before grabbing my growing cock and holding it tightly with her hand as she kisses my ball sack.

"Oh, fuck," I say as I look over and watch Tonya servicing Adrian. Her small fingers are massaging his balls as she siphons his cock. "This is so good," I moan as I look down at Chelsea. I run my fingers through her hair as I enjoy the light suction she is applying to my hard pole. I want very badly to turn her around and fuck her hard, but I know better. Oral sex is what is on offer for now, but I imagine there is a lot more if we decide to join the swingers club.

"I'm close," Adrian tells my wife. "If you can't catch it or swallow it, that's fine. Just point it away from my face, alright?" He laughs a little as he puts a hand on Tonya's head.

Chelsea lifts her head to tell her, "Adrian spurts hard, sweetie. If you can't take it, just back off, okay? He can shoot it several feet." Our host then looks at me, smiles, and goes back down on me.

"Oh, I'm about to explode," Adrian tells Tonya. "Be ready, alright? Be...*ohhhhhhhh...*" His body tenses suddenly but then relaxes slowly as he releases his first stream of jism into my wife's mouth.

"*Uttt...*" Tonya gags a little on the power of the spurt and the volume of semen coming out of the man. "*Ack...utttt...*" Some of his man gravy oozes from around her lips as she struggles to swallow it all. This makes me even harder as I feel Chelsea work diligently on my cock, ramming the head of it to the back of her throat.

"Fuck!" I say as I grind my ass into the chair. "Shit, I'm coming...*FUCK!!!*" I spurt hard as Chelsea draws my spunk into her mouth. "*Uhhh...uhhh...uhhh...*" My face becomes hot as I come over and over again. Her tongue continues to rake across my pisshole, causing me to lunge hard into her mouth. Chelsea has no problem swallowing my thick white gravy as I empty my balls into her throat.

"That was very nice," Adrian says to Tonya as he hands her a towel to clean her face. She does this as she turns and looks at me.

"Russ," she says quietly as she watches Chelsea pull her mouth from my cock. There is no semen left on me as she wipes her mouth lightly with her fingers.

"Was it okay?" I say to my wife as I look at her. "Are you okay?"

Tonya allows a strange smile as she chuckles. "That was a lot of stuff."

"I'm sorry," Adrian replies as he zips his pants. "I can't help it when I do that."

"He has larger balls and a higher sperm and semen production," Chelsea laughs. "I found this out when I gave him a blow job on our first date. I thought that I was going to drown from it."

I laugh. "Damn, what a problem to have."

"Well, it has been a problem a few times," Adrian offers. "It upsets some women when they find out unexpectedly."

"Not me," Tonya replies. "It was hard to swallow it all, but I got it down. I'm not a virgin, you know."

We all laugh. "No, apparently not," Chelsea replies. We continue to talk about the swingers club and it appears that Tonya becomes more comfortable with the idea. After all, she just gave another man that she had just met a great blow job. It would be easy to do so again, right?

"Thank you for the information," Tonya says a half-hour later as we are leaving the house. Chelsea and Adrian see us to the door and we are soon driving back home. I look over and see a slight smile on my wife's face.

"Are you good with this?" I ask her as I feel my body shiver from the excitement of what has just happened.

"You know what? I think I am, Russ. This was a pretty fun time." She smiles as we make our way through the city toward our own home. I was worried that Tonya would be absolutely against the idea when we went to see the managers of the club, but she has proven how ready she actually is for something new. This visit has opened up a huge opportunity for the two of us, and I am excited to see where it leads.

Chapter Six: Shocking But Not

"Well, it's been a while, girl," Treena laughs as I walk through her front door. "How have you been?"

I give my friend a quick hug before replying, "I have been great. How about you?"

Treena walks with me to the couch where we both have a seat. "I am doing okay as well. You haven't texted me back since the last time I messaged you, though." My blonde-haired bestie frowns as she looks accusingly at me. "Why have you been ignoring me, Tonya?"

"I'm sorry," I answer as I reach out and pat her on the knee. "Russ and I have been pretty busy with work and some other things."

"And some other things." Treena giggles. "That old boyfriend thing?"

"Uh, no. I told you that we broke that off, right? Marcus is with his wife and daughter and I have moved on. That was not something that was going to last forever."

"You took my advice," Treena says as she pats my hand. "I told you that it was time to close out that chapter of your life and to focus on your husband, Tonya. I'm glad to see that you actually listened to me." I do not offer any affirmation or denial to my friend's gloating claim, but she knew that my sexual relationship with Marcus would eventually come to an end. Anyone could have made that prediction if they had known me very well.

"So, how are things in the dating world for you?" I ask as I try to move the conversation away from my own love life.

Treena sighs. "Well, it's not been all that great. I've met a few guys but most of them have been complete duds. They want the same thing, Tonya; pussy without commitment."

I laugh. "You can't expect all guys to want to marry you right when they first meet you, Treena. Some of them want to try out the cow before they buy the milk." We both laugh together as I think about my friend's past sex life. She was married for a while to a man who was little better than a huge asshole and that has scarred her as far as affection for other men is concerned. I have wondered whether she might turn into a lesbian, but I have seen very little evidence of that yet. Treena still likes men, but she wants a particular type of man with a particular personality about him. I am not sure that one like that exists anymore.

"I just want a nice guy, you know? Someone who can be authentic with me and share the good times and the bad times. I'm not as picky as you think I am, Tonya, but I want what I want and I don't see why I have to settle." She smiles at me and asks, "What are you and Russ doing for fun now that Marcus is out of your life?" No matter what I do, my friend almost always seems to be able to move the conversation back to my own life.

"Well, we are looking at something a little less conventional. Russ contacted a swingers club and we went to look their place over."

"A *swingers* club?" Treena giggles. "Oh, my, that would be a lot of fun. Why are you looking at doing something like that?"

"Russ thinks that it would help to bring the spice back into the bedroom for us. Since Marcus and I have stopped have sex, things are a little less fun for the two of us." I shake my head as I think about how dry our sex life has become. At the moment, it is full of basic sex positions and agreed upon times to be intimate. The little hand job I gave Russ in the supermarket last week is the most adventurous we have been in quite some time.

"It probably would help to get things turned on between the two of you," Treena agrees. "I would love to look into something like that for myself, but then again I don't have a partner to take with me. They don't allow singles, I don't believe."

"No, they don't. But hey, that would be weird, right? If you were at the club for the same party as us and you had a boyfriend? You could screw Russ while I screw your boyfriend." I laugh and watch as Treena also breaks into laughter.

"Uh, *no.* Russ is yours and I have no interest, sweetie. I don't mean anything personally by that, but I don't think that I could ever strip down in front of him and do the nasty." We both begin to laugh again as Treena gets up from her seat. "I've got some cookies and tea made for us. I'll bring them out." My friend disappears into the kitchen as I settle back into the couch.

"It's crazy, right?" I say loudly to her while she is in the kitchen.

"The swinging thing? A little," Treena replies. "But it's whatever floats your boat, sweetie. The two of you need to figure out what it is that you really want and go for it no matter what anyone else has to say about it. I'm not a professional swinger, so I don't really know what to tell you about that. Do you like the idea of doing it?" My friend walks back into the living room with a tray of cookies along with two cups of hot tea.

After taking one of the cups from the tray, I reply, "I liked what I saw and heard while visiting there. The managers are very nice and they host all of the parties at a very nice home in an exclusive gated neighborhood. Honestly, all the images I had in my head about swingers parties sort of evaporated as they took us on a tour of the house. I liked everything about it."

"There is something else that you haven't told me," Treena says as she narrows her eyes at me. "What else is there about this place that has you convinced to go through with it?"

My heart races as I think about what happened in the living room between the four of us there. Treena, though, is my best friend. If I cannot be honest with her, who can I be honest with? "We gave the guys blow jobs," I reply flatly before taking a quick drink of my tea.

"Shit, really?" Treena almost spills her cup of tea before putting it back down on the tray. "You blew Russ in front of them?"

"Well, not exactly," I reply. "I gave a blow job to Adrian, the other man, and his wife Chelsea gave Russ head. Russ really seemed to liked it."

Wow, girl! Treena laughs as she shakes her head. Her eyes have lit up and she is now very interested in getting even more information about what happened during our visit. "How did it go?"

I nod my head. "Fine, I guess. Adrian has a weird condition where his balls are a little bigger and so he makes more semen. A *lot* more. I nearly puked on it as he came inside my mouth. It took a lot of effort to swallow it all."

"You *swallowed?* Did you know him before you went over there?"

"No," I reply.

"I never swallow the first time. I'm a spitter until I know a guy better," Treena laughs. "You actually sucked the guy off?" I nod my head again. "And Russ liked the woman?"

"Chelsea. Yeah, he came pretty hard as she sucked on him too. She swallowed for him and I thought he might up and elope with her right after. It was all he could talk about all the way home."

Treena studies my face. "And that is what worries you, huh? You are worried that Russ can't separate sex from a real relationship." I nod my head as I feel a chill run down my back. It is the sort of thing that I have thought about since getting home from the tour of the swingers house. Though I have agreed to join the club with Russ, I have not completely stopped worrying about what could happen as a consequence.

"He's a good man and I know he loves me more than anyone else, but Russ can sometimes be very weak when it comes to women. He was very tightly bonded to his old girlfriend in college and I thought he might still be having some kind of emotional affair with her up until sometime last year. I want to do this with him, but I don't want him to try to run off with another woman."

"He won't," Treena tells me. "I've seen how he is with you, Tonya. He loves you very much and he wants you to be happy. It's why he let the Marcus thing go on for so long. Honestly, I was more worried about you having feelings for your old boyfriend than I was about Russ looking for someone else for a relationship. You mean so much to him, girl."

"I know," I say with a sigh. "I'm being a little too paranoid, aren't I?" Treena nods her head. "I'll work on that."

"Good," she replies. "And work on those cookies on the plate." I smile as I pick up a cookie.

"When will you be going there for your first party?"

"I'm not sure yet," I tell her. "We are still working on that. We have to pay the dues and then get a date for the party. Chelsea and Adrian only invite about half of the couples at a time. They stagger the parties the couples can attend so that they don't all show up at the same time. Apparently they also want to shuffle who shows up each time so that eventually all couples get to know each other. They even encourage the couples to get together on their own if they can."

"Wow. What if they all want sex with each other at once?" Treena asks.

"They are not allowed to have orgies. They try to keep couples in bedrooms so that they can simply swap one for another. I told Russ that I would never do the orgy thing."

Treena smiles. "Like the guys you banged at the casino?"

"Oh, shit," I laugh. "Russ brought that up too when he was begging for this. That was not an orgy, Treena."

"Of course not." She winks at me as she brings her cup of tea to her lips. "Maybe you can find me a boyfriend there?" she laughs.

"And take him away from his wife or girlfriend?"

"I can offer more than most women, Tonya. Work it for me, girl!" We laugh and continue to enjoy our time together. I would love to find my friend a nice guy somehow, but her pickiness keeps her from actually accepting anyone that I suggest to her. There are lots of nice men who would be great for Treena, but she needs to change her attitude on dating before she finds one for herself. Spending this time with her causes me to count my blessings with my husband and his willingness to experiment sexually with me.

Sign up to my Patreon account and receive exclusive Hotwife stories every month and sexy scenes every week!

https://www.patreon.com/karlyviolet

Chapter Seven: An Agreement

After speaking with Treena yesterday afternoon, I began to wonder just what was going through my husband's mind as he got that blow job from Chelsea. With my curiosity finally getting the best of me, I decide to text Russ and ask him what he thought about our time at their house.

"Hey," I say in a text message to him. Though we are both at work, he tends to be able to respond to me quickly whenever I send him a text.

"Hey back," he says with a smiley face emoji. "What's going on, beautiful lady?" A smile forms on my face as I begin to type my reply.

"I was wondering, Russ. What did you really think of the way Chelsea gave you oral?" My skin prickles with goosebumps as I smile like a teenage girl in a naughty relationship with her boyfriend. Though I know that he loved it thoroughly, and he told me as much as we went home afterward, my husband has not really given me a full picture of what he liked about it.

"You know that it was good, right? I came because of it, honey." He sends a laughing emoji and I smile along with the cartoon effigy.

"Yeah, you did, but what was it like for you? What did you like about it while she was doing it? Tell me about it, Russ. Don't hold anything back." My heart beats hard inside my chest as I await his response. I want to hear it all, even if something could cause me to worry about our marriage. Does he feel some sort of love for Chelsea after she received his cock into her mouth and swallowed his jism? I have to ask.

"She really used her tongue," he replies after a moment. "Chelsea ran it over the end of my dick and then under it several times. What she did was really intense."

"Did she suck you hard?" I ask as I try to understand how this experience was so different than what I have given Russ before. I cannot help but feel slightly jealous of the way Chelsea made him feel during the oral sex she gave him that afternoon.

"Not at first," he answers. "She was very slow to begin with but then she slowly ramped it up. She also spent some time on my balls."

"Yeah, you told me about your balls as we rode home after seeing them. I lick your balls, Russ," I tell him as I feel hurt by the way he apparently liked the way she licked them for him. "You like the way I do that for you, right?"

"Honey, I love your blow jobs," he says quickly. "Is that what this is all about? Are you jealous of Chelsea? It was just a blow job. I swear."

"I keep telling myself that," I say after pausing for a moment to collect my thoughts. "But you really liked what she did to you, huh? I want to be that for you too. I want you to be able to tell others that I am the best oral sex you have ever had."

"Oh." The one-worded response is all I get for a couple of minutes before he adds, "Tonya, you have nothing to worry about. It was just a blow job. I'm not going to run off and marry Chelsea or anything like that. You and I are together, right? I love you and only you, baby." I feel better as I read his text message, but there is still something that bothers me about the whole thing. I am surprised when the next message from Russ comes through my phone.

"Tell me about that blow job you gave Adrian. What did it taste like?"

"What?" I laugh to myself as I think about the question my husband poses. "I don't know. It was sort of salty and a little like okra, I think."

"Okra?" I imagine Russ laughing as he adds several humorous emojis in his message to me. "When have you had okra?"

"I grew up on a farm," I remind him. "We ate okra sometimes."

"Alright. Salty okra." Again, there are laughing emojis that pop up on my cell phone screen. Russ seems to be having a good time with this. "And how much did he come inside your mouth? It seemed like a lot."

"It was a lot," I answer back. "Russ, it had to be more than twice the amount of semen that I have ever had inside my mouth. And he came so hard too. I gagged on it."

"I saw you gag," he replies. "Did you like giving that blow job to Adrian?"

I sit back in my desk chair and think about the question. Though I almost vomited, I did enjoy knowing that I made him orgasm like that. Each powerful spurt of warm, salty semen nearly caused me to throw up my stomach contents, but they also let me know that I had done my job very well. Adrian liked the blow job I gave him and I am proud of that fact.

"I liked it," I admit to my husband.

"Are you in love with him?"

"No, silly," I answer back.

"Then why would you think that I am somehow in love with Chelsea after getting a blow job from her?"

"You know why," I answer.

"Dammit, Tonya, don't judge me based on a relationship that I had with a woman years ago in college. I'm not with her at this moment, right? I'm with you. I will always be with you." Though I feel that Russ is scolding me through his text messages, I understand his frustration. I have for a long time thought that he would be unable to have a simple sexual relationship with another woman. He fell hard for a woman in his college days and the breakup was devastating for him. Russ has told me more than once how he thought she was the one to marry when she broke his heart. Even after meeting me, it took just a couple of dates for Russ to tell me that he was madly in love with me and wanted to be with me forever. I remember how it scared me at first, but then I came to appreciate how eager he was to share his heart with me.

"I need to work on that," I tell him. "I will. I promise. Just promise me that when we go to a party at the club you will not fall in love with anyone."

"I swear to it," Russ replies with a serious looking emoji following. "You can't get rid of me that easily, honey. You and I are glued together."

"Good!" I send several kissing emojis to my husband and smile to myself. I love him so much and yet I want to have these sexual experiences with him. I want to see how he will be with another woman in bed.

"Be good. I need to get back to work, alright? See you after work."

"After work. I love you, Russ!"

"I love you too." We end our text conversation and I lay my phone down on my desk. Though I am having a difficult time seeing him as someone who can separate his physical horniness from a need for love, I have to begin to try. I owe it to Russ as well as to myself if this swinging thing is going to work out.

There is a knock at my open office door and I look up to see Landon Smith, a coworker of mine from down the hallway. "Can I come in a moment?" he asks.

"Sure." He walks in with a manila folder in his hand. He hands it over to me. "What's this?"

He sighs. "We are looking at possibly adding a couple of additional positions in sales and advertising and I was hoping that you could look at the numbers to see if you think it will pass management's smell test."

I smile. "So, the higher-ups didn't ask for this information?"

Landon shakes his head. "Well, no. We need the extra help, though, so I am hoping to convince them with our own research on how it will eventually mean a greater profit margin for the company."

Landon is a handsome young man, around thirty years old and very athletic. His light brown hair and hazel eyes are attractive and cause my heart to palpitate occasionally. There is not a woman in this company who would not enjoy feeling his young, studly body between her legs. I count myself in that group.

Moving around in my seat and feeling the wetness forming between my labia, I ask, "When are you going to give this to them?"

"Early next week," he replies. "Can you look it over? I would appreciate your opinion on whatever we need to polish up. They seem to like you upstairs."

I laugh. "Well, I know how to keep my head down and do my job. This is not the sort of thing that I would normally put my name on."

"It won't be on it," Landon promises. "I just want your opinion and any changes you think that I should make. I'll take any and all heat if there is any." He smiles at me and I feel a tingle in my breasts. I wish I could close my office door and just let him fuck me.

"I'll look at it," I say with a smile. "But you need to bring your girlfriend by my house sometime to have dinner with my husband and I."

Landon nods and smiles, but informs me, "I don't have a girlfriend right now."

"No girlfriend? I thought you were seeing someone here?"

"She was just a date for one night," he says to me. "There was really nothing that came out of it." I think about how stupid that woman must be. I do not know her, though, as she works in another part of the company. Surely she was not completely blind and could see just how attractive the young man is.

"I'm sorry to hear that," I say as I think about sex with Landon. "You should find you someone who is looking for a nice guy like you. Do you know of anyone else that you might be interested in?"

"Not really," he says with a slight frown. "I don't have time to go out and look for women to date, though. I'm good on my own for now. Work takes up a lot of my time anyway."

Suddenly, an idea comes to mind. "I have this friend," I begin as I reach for a pad of paper on top of my desk. "Her name is Treena and she hasn't been in a relationship for a while."

"For a while?" I get the sense from Landon that he is already worried as to why she has not had a boyfriend in some time.

"She's picky," I tell him. "She wants someone who is nice and won't be too quick to try to get her into bed. You seem like a nice guy for her, Landon." I write down my friend's name on a piece of paper as well as her phone number. After tearing it off the pad, I hand it to the young man.

"You should call her and tell her that I gave you her number. She would love to hear from you."

"Are you sure?" he asks as he arches an eyebrow.

"Definitely," I assure him. "She is really a nice lady and she wants to find a great guy who can be caring and gentle with her. So, call her. If it doesn't work out, what harm has been done, right? I promise that you won't be sorry."

He takes the small piece of paper from me and nods his head. "Thanks. I'll call her." Smiling, Landon takes one last look at the folder on my desk before turning and walking out of my office. I sit back in my seat and think about how nice and firm his ass must be. Treena will thank me for this. At least, she had better.

Chapter Eight: A Former Fling

Tonya has always worried that I might find another woman, fall in love, and leave her. I have had trouble understanding that, but my wife has it set in her mind that if I have sex with someone else it could mean that I am going to leave her for that woman. If only I could prove to her that could never be the case. Unfortunately, I sometimes wonder whether she is right. Tonya has made viable arguments that I was deeply in love with my ex-girlfriend Sandra. She was right. I loved Sandra very much and hoped to marry her one day, but things changed for me when I met Tonya. Though I am no longer in love with my former girlfriend, I do think about her occasionally. I cannot help but do this because we were at one time in love.

"Why are you doing this?" I ask myself as I sit in my car in the parking lot at work. I have made certain to move to a shaded part of the lot where I am less likely to be seen by other company minions. "You're asking for a shit storm if Tonya finds out, Russ." I ignore my own warnings as I get on Facebook and message Sandra. I want to know some things about our time together so that I can better understand my wife's concerns.

"Sandra, it's the old boyfriend," I type in the messenger box to her as I smile. I can see that she is logged on, but that does not mean that she is going to see the message anytime soon. Lots of people stay logged into their accounts without being directly on the site.

"Russell?" For the first time in more than five years, Sandra and I make contact.

"Yeah, it's me. How are you doing?"

"Wait, is this a joke? Russell? *My Russell?*"

I laugh. "Well, not *your* Russell anymore. Also, I go by Russ now."

My phone suddenly rings and I answer it. "You will always be my Russell," I hear a familiar voice say over the line.

"*What?!*" I sit back in my car seat. "How did you get my phone number, Sandra?"

She giggles. "It's on your account, Russell. You need to take that down. People no longer make that sort of information public. There are too many creeps out there." I smile as I hear her laugh again. It has been so long since I have heard Sandra laugh that I have forgotten just how much I loved it.

"I will have to remember to do that," I say as I move around in my seat. "How have you been?"

"I've been great," she replies. "How about you? You're going by Russ now, huh?"

"I'm good and yes."

"Russ. I guess that makes sense. Maybe I should have called you that back when we were dating?" We both enjoy a short laugh before Sandra asks, "Why are you messaging me, Russ?"

Swallowing hard first, I answer, "I have a question or two about when you and I were together in college, if you are willing to go along with it. There are things in my marriage to Tonya now that have come up because you and I were a thing."

"Really? What sort of problems?"

"Trust problems," I reply. "I'm completely faithful to her, Sandra, but Tonya is worried that I might become too attached to another woman if I get to know her too well. She says that I tend to become very emotionally connected very quickly. So, I thought I would ask you..."

"Yes, Russ," my ex-girlfriend interrupts. "You get very emotionally tied in with a woman if you get too close to her." I sit motionless in my car as I consider her response.

"Are you sure? I mean, I'm not talking about finding a woman and seriously dating her, but just knowing a woman as a friend or acquaintance can get me into some trouble with Tonya."

"She has good reason to worry," Sandra replies. "Russell...Russ...you are a great guy. You always worried about what I wanted and how you could fix things for me, but it started that way from the first time we met. We hadn't even had a date yet and you were already sitting near me at that concert as if you were protecting me. Honestly, you became a little suffocating after we started dating."

"But, we had a great time with each other, right?" I feel a little stung by Sandra's commentary on my past relationship with her. "I loved you, but you also loved me."

"Sure, I loved you," she replies. "But I was not into the idea of marrying you. We dated less than a year before you started telling me that you wanted to marry me, Russ. I know that there are lots of girls who would have loved that, but you and I were not ready to marry yet. I'm not sure that we ever would have been."

"Yeah, you said that when you broke up with me." The same heaviness in my heart that I felt years ago I am beginning to feel right now. Losing Sandra the way that I did took time to heal from. As of right now, I still carry the scars of that broken relationship.

"I didn't mean to hurt you, Russ. You know that I didn't, right?" It almost seems that there is something still unresolved for Sandra as well as she asks me the question.

I sigh. "Yeah, I know. It was a tough time for us both. I just wish that I could have seen the way I was being with you. I could have treated you better than I did."

"Oh, no, you treated me like a queen," she replies with a laugh. "That was the problem, Russ. You loved me *too* much. It scared me. So, I did the only thing that I could do. I broke up with you and moved on." Sandra pauses before asking, "Do you still hold a flame for me, Russell?" It is the sort of question that I did not expect to answer when I messaged my old girlfriend on Facebook.

"There are still feelings," I admit.

"And you would take me back right now?"

"Well...no. I'm with Tonya now."

"Then that is what she needs to hear from you, sweetheart. She needs to know that you are not going to leave her for me or for anyone else.

Keep telling her that and convince her. Don't allow her to think that there is any way that you would leave her."

"That makes sense," I reply. "I have tried doing it like that, but I'm not sure just how far I have gotten with her that way. She's still pretty resistant to believing me."

"Then make her see it, Russ. Don't allow that to sit and fester. Show your wife that you love her only." A chill runs along my neck as I continue to listen to the sweet voice of my old girlfriend. There is no longer true love between us, but I still lust for her sexually. If I had the opportunity to do so, I might be willing to fuck Sandra again. Sex was great with her and very adventurous, but it also meant a very different thing to me than it did to her. That became obvious after we broke up.

"I'll do that," I promise. "Thanks for talking to me, Sandra. You have been very helpful."

"Hey, that's what an old girlfriend is for, right?" She laughs before adding, "And I'm not married anymore, so if you ever want to come over and relive some of the things we used to do together, feel free."

The offer causes another chill to run along my neck and back. "Are you saying..."

"Yes, Russ. I would love to have sex with you if you ever want to come by just to have a little fun. I'll text you my address just in case you ever want to come over. Don't tell your wife, though, alright? This would just be between us." My cock becomes erect as I struggle to know what to say in response to the offer from my ex-girlfriend.

"Alright," I say as I feel my heart pounding inside my chest. "I'll keep that in mind."

"Good." Sandra and I say goodbye and hang up from the phone call. I look around the parking lot and consider what she said and my reaction to it. Tonya is right. I do find myself easily attached to other women.

"Dammit," I mutter as I adjust myself in the seat of my car. Leaning my seat back, I unzip my pants and pull out my cock. It is so hard now that my balls are aching and I need relief quickly. I want to shoot my wad.

"Yes," I say under my breath as I rub my cock with both hands. I look at the picture of Sandra on the website and consider how sexy she still is. "I wish I could fuck you in the ass," I tell her as I look at my cell phone. "I would come hard inside you, baby." My body begins to tense with the expectation of the imminent orgasm.

"Oh, fuck," I say loudly as I look around the car. "Fuck, I'm going to...*SHIT!*" I spurt hard into the air and some of my jism lands on the steering wheel in front of me. *"Sandra...fuck...SANDRA!!!* I come hard as I think about her pink, soft pussy lips wrapped tightly around my shaft. She was always such a good lay when I was with her. My former girlfriend kept her nether region waxed and smooth, ready for me to play in it whenever I wanted to. Her asshole bleached, we also spent time enjoying anal sex as well. I miss that time with Sandra, but I do not love her anymore. I keep telling myself that quietly as I finish coming in my hands.

"Dammit, Russ," I complain as I look for something to wipe my mess up. "You are fucking out of your damned mind." Tonya would not approve if she knew that I had spoken to Sandra. She would approve even less if she knew that I was offered sex by her. That little piece of information will never be shared with my wife by me. I just wish that I had thought better than to have called Sandra in the first place. Now I will have a hard time getting her out of my mind.

My phone buzzes. It is a text message from Chelsea. "I look forward to seeing you both here for our little party this weekend. Hopefully we will get to take things a little further then." A pair of lips follow the message and I shake my head as I laugh.

"Wow, you need to focus on Tonya and what you are doing with her this weekend, man. Forget Sandra. There are other things that you need to do now." I find a few napkins and clean up my mess before putting my cock back and zipping my pants. Turning on the car, I decide that I will go get something cold to drink before I head home. I need something that will cool me off before I see Tonya. The last thing I want is for her to figure out what I have done this afternoon.

Chapter Nine: Sharing the Spouse

"Here we are," I say to Tonya with a smile as we drive up to the large home owned by Adrian and Chelsea. "It's good to be here finally." As we pull close to the front door, a young man comes out and takes the keys to our car. "They have valets," I tell my wife with a chuckle.

"Your thousand dollars at work," she quips as I walk over to her. "I hope this is worth it."

"Me too," I say nervously as we make our way into the large home. Since talking to Sandra the day before yesterday, I have worried that I might accidentally say her name in my sleep. It would not be a good thing to blurt out my ex-girlfriend's name in front of my current wife.

We walk up to the door and are allowed inside by a young man with a leather-bound notepad. As we make our way through the foyer, Adrian and Chelsea meet us. "Hello and welcome to you both," Chelsea says with a warm smile. "I am so glad to see that you are here. Please come in and help yourself to a drink. Mingle as you like and have fun." She pats me on the shoulder before she turns and walks away with her husband.

"I guess we are on our own," I say as I look around. "Where should we begin?"

Tonya shrugs her shoulders. "I don't know. Maybe the bar?" My wife nods her head toward a bar that is sitting at one end of the living room. We make our way there and have the bartender make a drink for each of us. Sitting down on a stool beside the bar, Tonya asks, "Is this the way it will be all night? Dance music playing and drinks? This might not be so bad." She takes a sip of the margarita in her hand as I nurse a bottle of cold beer.

"I'm sure things will get going eventually," I reply. "These people are not here to just socialize all night. They want to have sex."

Tonya frowns. "They want to make connections with other couples before they do. Maybe we should try to do the same, Russ." My wife looks around and begins to move away from the bar as someone walks up to us.

"Hello, Tonya," a familiar voice says to her.

"Treena?" My wife seems shocked as she sees her friend in the swingers club. "What are you doing here?"

"Um, well, I decided to bring a date to this thing." Treena motioned toward a young man with her. I watch as Tonya's eyes become wide.

"Landon?" Her face red, I wonder what this man is to her.

"I'm Russ," I say to him as I offer my hand.

"I know," he replies as he shakes it. "I work for the same company as you, not far from where Tonya works."

"You actually called her?" My wife still seems completely shocked that the two of them are here. I feel pretty weird myself as I look at Treena, a woman who is not someone I know much about but I have seen around before.

"I called her," Landon tells her as he nods his head. "I didn't know that she was going to invite me to a party on the first date, though."

"A party?" Tonya looks at her friend. "Just a party date?"

"Yeah, *just* a party date." Treena looks hard at my wife. "You know how parties can be, right? They can sometimes get a little wild and fun. That's all this is, Tonya. A *party.*"

"Oh, okay." Tonya nods her head and giggles. "Um, it's a nice party, huh?" I finally understand what is going on here as I watch the two women together. Landon has no clue what is supposed to happen here.

"Hey, do you want to get a beer with me, Landon? We can talk and let the ladies spend some time together." I smile at my wife's coworker as he nods his head and moves toward me. "Don't worry, Treena. He's in good hands." I wink at Tonya's friend as I turn around and step toward the bar with him.

"Do you know Treena?" he asks as we stand in front of the bar waiting for the bartender.

"Yeah, I know her a little. She's Tonya's best friend. I guess you were introduced by my wife to her?"

"With a phone number," he replies. "Tonya said that I should call her and take her out. Treena wanted to come here for our first date." The young man looks around at all the people in the room. "I don't recognize anyone here."

"Didn't you meet Chelsea and Adrian?"

"Who?"

"Oh." I look over at Treena. "She must have signed you both up on her own. Normally the hosts like to meet the guests before they come over for a party."

He nods his head. "She mentioned that she met someone and got an invitation. It's a nice party." Landon looks around the room again and I think about the one thousand dollars Treena had to put up just to bring Landon here.

"Hey, let's go sit somewhere and talk, alright?" Treena leads all four of us down a hallway and into one of the bedrooms. We sit down on the two large beds as my wife's friend shakes her head. "Landon, I have to be honest now that we are here." Her dark eyes look up at him.

"Alright." He looks confused as he sits forward on the edge of the bed.

Treena looks nervously at Tonya before she tells her date, "This isn't a regular party, Landon. I didn't tell you everything there is to know about this place."

"Okay." He looks questioningly at her. "Then what do I need to know?"

My wife swallows hard as she looks at her friend's face. This is proving difficult for Treena to tell Landon. "What she is trying to say is that this party is by invitation only and it's not a normal party. Only couples are invited." Tonya smiles uneasily as she studies the man's face.

"Only *couples*?"

"For a reason," I chime in. "There is something that happens between couples here." I wave my hands around to hint at our surroundings. Landon looks around as his eyes become large.

"Wait, are you saying this is a *sex* party?"

"A swingers party," Tonya replies. "There is sometimes sex involved." Her face is a little pink as she looks at her coworker.

"You didn't tell me that I was signing up for a swingers thing, Treena," Landon tells his date. "Why didn't you tell me?"

Her face flushed, Treena answers him. "I'm sorry. I don't know what I was thinking, honestly. I just wanted to go out with you and this seemed like something fun to do. I don't think I really planned out doing this and then having sex with someone, but I get that you are probably pretty angry with me."

He shakes his head. "I'm confused, not angry," he says. Landon looks at Tonya and asks, "Are you and your husband swingers?"

"Our first time," Tonya admits as her face becomes even redder. "I didn't know that my friend and her date would be showing up tonight, though." My wife laughs nervously as she looks from the young man to Treena. My cock gets a little hard as I see the sexual tension between Landon and my wife.

"You are welcome to stay," I tell him. "There are people looking for sex if you are interested."

Landon shudders as he replies, "I don't know how to even begin. I've never done anything like this before."

Tonya gets up from where she is sitting and walks over to him. She puts a hand on his shoulder before leaning in and kissing him. "Oh, shit," I say as I feel my cock pre-come a little inside my pants.

"What are you doing, Tonya?" her friend asks as she watches the two of them begin to feel each other's bodies.

"She wants him," I tell Treena as I watch the two of them together. "Tonya wants Landon and it appears that he wants her too." My wife reaches down and begins to unfasten his pants. As she does, Treena sits quietly nearby and watches.

"Tonya," Landon moans as she fishes his cock out of his pants. She begins to run her hands over his swelling meat as she nibbles on his ball sack. "I can't believe that this is happening," he says breathlessly as he enjoys my wife's lips and tongue on his scrotum.

"I can't believe it either," Treena says with disappointment as she watches them. It is obvious that she had planned to have sex with Landon tonight.

I get up from where I am sitting and go over to Treena. "Undo my pants," I say to her as I look down into her eyes.

"Ew, Russ," she complains. "I'm your wife's friend."

"Tonight, you are one of a couple, Treena. My wife and your date are going to have sex. Why should we be left out?" I want her to open my pants and pull out my cock for me. I do not want to have her say later that I pressured her into anything. Treena is an attractive woman and I have been horny for her before. Her attitude toward me at times has been a bit cold, but I can look past that to fuck her.

Treena slowly reaches for my zipper. Her fingers grip it and she slowly opens my pants. "I don't think this is a good idea, Russ. You are married to Tonya."

"I know," I say as I look down at her and smile. "And you have needs, right? We both do." I watch patiently as Treena reaches into my pants and finds my hard cock waiting for her. Treena pulls it out and looks at it, her eyes affixed on the tip of it. A small drip of pre-come is oozing from my pisshole as I yearn to feel her mouth on it. "Take it into your mouth, Treena. Suck it."

She looks at me and grimaces before slowly opening her lips and allowing my penis to slide into her mouth. Tonya looks over to see this and smiles before she goes back down on Landon. I close my eyes and just enjoy the silky sensation of the inside of her mouth.

"Can we watch?" Chelsea and Adrian come into the bedroom and walk up to us.

"Sure," I moan as Treena begins to really enjoy what she is doing to me. I put my hand on her head and relax as I let her do all the work.

Chelsea moves behind Landon and helps him take off his dress shirt. She then backs away as Tonya helps him get his pants off. It does not take long for my wife to lower her naked body down on top of his long, hard cock as he lays on the bed. "Shit, Landon," she moans as she carefully allows her pussy to slide down. "You're fucking long!"

"You're tight," he replies. "So fucking tight, Tonya." His pelvis grinds beneath Tonya as she moves around on top of him, her small breasts and pink nipples quaking with each motion.

"Here." Treena stands to her feet and pulls her small dress over her head. She is wearing no bra or panties, her dark, hard nipples suddenly staring at me as she drops her dress to the floor. "Fuck me hard, Russ. I have wanted you to do that for as long as I have known you." My manhood flexes hard as I hear her admit that to me. After she lays back on the bed, I pull down my pants and push the head of my cock hard against her pink pussy. Treena is already wet and expecting me as I slide into her.

"Oh, shit," I groan as I feel how tight she is. "Treena, you are so...*fuck*." I push her legs back and can feel her firm cervix down low. I press my cock hard against it and watch her toes point. She feels me deep inside her and it makes me hornier than I have ever been.

Chelsea undresses, as does Adrian, and they begin to play with each other. Her breasts are large with pink nipples and her kitty is trimmed with a strip of hair. I smile as I think about fucking her. I want to fuck her, but Treena's twat is too much for me to leave. I have to come inside her.

"Oh...Landon..." Tonya leans back as she rides the young man's johnson. His hands move around on her chest as he massages her small orbs. The two lovers are deep into their fuckery as they wriggle around on the bed together. "Oh, Landon...*uhhh*..." My wife squeals as she orgasms with him deep inside her pussy. *"OHHHHH!!!"* She then shrieks out as her body shudders on top of Landon's. Though he has yet to come, Landon's cock has made it easy for her to do so.

Treena taps my arm. "Let me turn around." I pull out of her and she turns around, her ass in the air. I push into her again and watch as her puckered back door flexes as I continue to fuck her pussy. "Finger my ass," she groans as she feels me stroke it a couple of times with a fingertip. "Please."

"Let me," I hear Chelsea say. She licks her finger and then pushes it into Treena's tight asshole.

"Oh, yes. Finger me."

Chelsea moves her finger in and out of her quickly. "There you go. Is that good?" The moaning from Treena as I fuck her in the pussy and our host plays with her ass lets us know that she likes what is happening. Chelsea then pulls me toward her and kisses me hard, her tongue finding mine quickly.

I pull away after a moment and look at her. "Shit, this is real, huh?"

"Yeah, it is." Chelsea smiles at me as I get closer to coming inside Treena.

"Shit," the woman beneath me says. "I'm ovulating, I think. You need a condom."

"No," I say as I begin to go over the top. "What the fuck, Treena? Why would you come here if you think you're fucking fertile?" The admission makes me even hornier. I suddenly begin to come inside her tight, wet snapper. *FUCK!!! FUCK!!! FUCK!!!*" I bury my manhood deep inside her as I shower her open cervix with my genetic soup. *"Ohhh...fuck...I'll get you pregnant!!! SHIT!!!"* I pound her pussy hard as my balls crash against her labia. If I had known how tight Treena was before, I would have tried to screw her long ago.

I turn to see Landon pulling at my wife. It is his turn and he wants to come. He pushes his cock into her as he bends her over the bed and begins to thrust so hard that he moves the bed. "Dammit, I'm close," he yells into the air. "Fuck, I want you so bad, Tonya. I want to come inside you."

"Shit, Landon," Tonya replies as she hangs on. *"AHHHH!!!"* She comes for a second time as her lover begins to spray her womb with his spunk.

"NAHHHH!!! Fuck...uhhh...uhhh...uhhhhhh..." He pushes deep into her as his balls squash against her nay-nay. The young man empties himself into my wife's hole and I enjoy watching it all. I almost don't notice that Chelsea has gone to her knees and taken hold of my wet cock.

"Shit, Chelsea!" She sucks me into her mouth as I look down.

"She's cleaning you off," Adrian tells me before he presses his face against Treena's muff.

"Ohhhhh..." Treena's toes point as the older man feeds on her wet pussy. His tongue moves directly over her puffy clit as he pleasures her. Her hand goes down to his head as she lets Adrian bring her to an orgasm. *"AHHHH!!!"* Her petite body quivers as he puts two fingers inside her wet hole and plays with her. His tongue continues to dance on top of her clitoris. *"Fuck, yes! FUCK, yes!!!"* The bed shakes hard as Adrian gives Treena the release that she so badly needs. To my surprise, I begin to come for the second time as Chelsea siphons my cock.

"Holy SHIT!!!" My balls ache as I pump semen I didn't know that I had left into her mouth. I pull hard on her head, stuffing my cock into the back of her throat. She gags a little, but I keep her pulled toward me as I keep coming. *"FUCK! Oh, shit, Chelsea...oh, TONYA!!!"* I look over at where she is resting on the bed. She is watching this all with great interest as I come for the second time. *"Ohhhh..."*

I soon finish orgasming and Chelsea backs away from me. Her face is red after being gagged by me, but I can tell that she is quite happy that I have given her something to swallow. We are all quiet for a time before dressing and going our separate ways, and I wonder what Tonya will make of this in the morning. For me, I am not quite sure how this all happened the way that it did. It will take some time for my mind to process it all.

Chapter 10: A New Chapter

71

I get on top of Russ and begin to move up and down his hard cock. He has been pawing at me all night and I am tired of having to fight him. So, I fuck him to hopefully get some sleep later on.

"You little whore," he growls at me as he carefully takes my breasts into his hands. My husband is so gentle with me during sex sometimes that I want to slap him and tie him to the bed. Hopefully he will eventually grow out of being so careful with me.

"I'm your little *whore?*" I ask playfully. "What does that make you, Russ? My *pimp?*" We both laugh as he pulls me down to his side and he rolls on top of me. His cock is right back inside me quickly as he puts my feet back and fucks me deep. "Oh, Russ, it's my G-spot," I tell him. "Right there. Keep going." He moves hard against me, the end of his long cock rubbing me just right.

"Tonya, I'm about to pop," he warns me. "Oh, hell, I'm...*ohhhhhhh...*" Russ dumps his sperm into me as he slowly thrusts in and out of my hole. He keeps rubbing my G-spot with his cock and I hope that he will not suddenly stop. I need my husband to keep doing this to me. I want to come too.

"RUSS!!!" My body shivers as I feel the intense sensation of an orgasm move through my abdomen and into my pussy. *"FUCK! That's ITTTT!!! Ohhhh..."* I grit my teeth a little as I enjoy the sensation of coming with my husband's cock deep inside me. This is the sort of thing that Marcus at one time did for me. Knowing that now I can get the same thing from Russ makes me very happy.

Russ rolls off of me after a minute or so and asks, "Was that good, honey?"

I roll toward him and reply, "Pretty damned good, dear. You actually found it."

"About fucking time," he laughs as he runs his fingers through my hair. "All I want is to make you happy, Tonya. You know that, right?"

I smile at him. "I know you do. That's what I want to do for you too." We kiss for a while as we simply enjoy each other's presence in bed. I love lying next to Russ this way and he seems to enjoy it just as much. This is the sort of thing that I was worried he would want with another woman. Thankfully, he has not mentioned Treena or Chelsea at all.

"You know, we will have to go back there sometime. We paid a lot of money for that membership so we need to get our worth out of it."

I giggle. "There will be another party on the twenty-second that we are invited to attend. Should we plan to go?" Russ nods his head at me as his finger traces one of my areolas. "You are being a very naughty man."

"I can be," he laughs. "Just ask your friend."

"Oh, wow. And here I thought that you weren't going to go there," I laugh as I look into Russ's eyes.

"It was fun," he tells me. "She wants to see me again, Tonya." My husband's expression changes and I can tell that he is not joking around with me.

"What?"

"She texted me and asked. I told her that I would have to ask you if that would be alright. Treena is fine if you want to be there, but she wants to have sex again with me. She apparently really liked it."

"Russ." I raise an eyebrow. "You two barely got along before you met at that party."

He laughs. "That means that you don't have to worry about me falling for her, right? I just want her body, baby. So, what do you say? Can I fuck your best friend again?"

Russ's dirty humor causes me to laugh along with him before I reply, "Yeah, I think that would be okay. I want to watch, though. I might want to join in too."

"What?" My husband's eyes widen a little as he looks at me.

"You heard me. I might want to make this a threesome or something. I'm not sure yet."

"Fuck, yeah." Russ smiles wide at the thought of two naked women with him in bed.

"Don't get too excited yet, Russ. I'm not sure that you understand just how difficult it could be to have the two of us in bed together. We are both hard to please."

My husband pulls me toward him and reaches down. One of his fingers moves over my wet clitoris as he smiles at me. "I think I know what to do with you."

"That's pretty twisted, sweetheart," I say as I begin to feel horny again. "Are you saying that you want to play with both of our clits?"

"I really do," he laughs. "I want to fuck you both, too. I'll pull out of you, enter Treena, then go back into you until you both come."

I scrunch my nose and laugh. "You are a disgusting man sometimes, Russ. You want to give us each sloppy seconds?" He smiles and kisses me again as he plays with my twat. His raw interest in the both of us turns me on again as I move around in his arms.

"And what will we do after that?" he asks me. "What are we going to do in our marriage? Are we just going to go to the parties and swing? Or is there something else?"

I shrug my shoulders. "I don't know. Maybe an open marriage or something like that?"

Russ's eyes light up again. "Seriously?"

"Maybe," I laugh. "Let's just take this thing one day at a time, okay? We will start with Treena and go from there."

"Yes!" Russ is excited as I confirm that we will go see my friend.

"After that, we will see where our interests take us. I would love to do some things that we have not done before, Russ. Maybe we could find safe, fun ways to do those things."

"Maybe we can," he replies. "Maybe we can." We lean in toward each other and begin to kiss again as Russ plays with my wet hole and I massage his hardening cock. It is going to be round two for us today, but I can see where there will be so much more for us soon. We love each other and only want the best in our marriage. It seems that the best includes experimenting sexually with ourselves and others.

THE END

THE END

Don't miss out!

Visit the website below and you can sign up to receive emails whenever Karly Violet publishes a new book. There's no charge and no obligation.

https://books2read.com/r/B-A-GIXE-TXAKB

BOOKS 2 READ

Connecting independent readers to independent writers.

Did you love *Hotwife to Swingers - A Multiple Partner Hotwife Romance Novel*? Then you should read *Wife Swapping Party - A Wife Watching Multiple Partner Hotwife Romance Novel*[1] by Karly Violet!

[2]

Imagine joining a new neighbourhood and welcomed into their warm Swinging community!

Jake and Marty recently moved into an exclusive adulted gated community in an affluent area.

Surrounded by wealth and beautiful people, their neighbours intrigued them - with endless flirting and over friendlessness.

The married couple read this as a welcome and supportive community that came with it's members having financial security. .

However, as Jake starts to learn more from his next door neighbours, it is clear there is more than meets the eyes.

---

1. https://books2read.com/u/31KPk6

2. https://books2read.com/u/31KPk6

There are hints of naughty parties centered around keys involving swinging and wife swapping.

And when curiosity gets the better of Jake..........

....and it's not long before husband and wife open the door to the world of swinging and multiple partners!

This scorching hot 20,000 word novel features a curious married couple exploring the virtues of swinging and wife swapping with their exclusive gated community.

Read more at https://www.patreon.com/karlyviolet.

About the Author

Sign up to my mailing list to receive the two free epilogues for 'A Hotwife Adventure' and 'Hotwife Training' and to stay up to date on all of my latest releases! http://eepurl.com/c3ICWf Sign up to my Patreon account and receive exclusive Hotwife stories every month and sexy scenes every week! https://www.patreon.com/karlyviolet

Read more at https://www.patreon.com/karlyviolet.

About the Publisher